MARGARET CARTER
and
CAROL WRIGHT

Go Away,

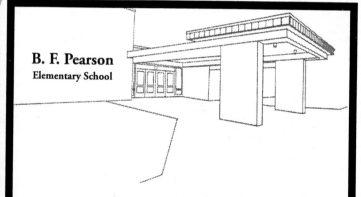

B. F. Pearson
Elementary School

Donated By: Mrs. Swanson

In Honor Of:

School Year: 1996-1997

William is a cat
who loves people.

He loves people so much
that he always wants
to be with them.

Sometimes he gets
in their way.

Then they say,
"Oh, do go away, William."

Then William is sad.

When Granny sews,
William gets in
the basket.

"Oh, do go away, William,"
says Granny.

When Father types,
William watches
anxiously.

"Oh, doo ga away, William!!!,"

says Father.

When Rose gardens,
William helps.

"OH, DO GO AWAY, WILLIAM,"

says Rose.

William

climbs into bookcases,

creeps into cupboards,

hides under beds,

stands with umbrellas.

"Go away, William," they all say.

William is sad.

"Where can I go?
I want to be
with people."

And then one day he hears,

" *William,*

William,

WILLIAM!"

William comes running.

"Look what we've got
for you, William,"
they say.

"Just for you,
next to the fire,
near all the people you love…

…your very own bed,
because we love you too
and want you near us…

…and not *always*
getting in our way!"

First published in Great Britain in 1989 by Methuen Children's Books Ltd, London. First American edition 1989.

Printed and bound by MacLehose & Partners, England.

10 9 8 7 6 5 4 3 2 1

Library of Congress Cataloging-in-Publication Data
Carter, Margaret. Go away, William. Summary: William the cat loves people so much that he gets in their way until they figure how he can always be around without becoming a nuisance. [1. Cats—Fiction] I. Wright, Carol (Carol S.) II. Title. PZ7.C2463Go 1989   [E]   88-8314
ISBN 0-02-717791-2